A Tale from Zanzibar

BIMWILI & THE ZIMWI

retold by Verna Aardema / *pictures by* Susan Meddaugh

Dial Books for Young Readers

New York

To my grandson Stevie Dufford who is a tagalong for his big brother, Danny.
V. A.

For H.
S. M.

Published by Dial Books for Young Readers
A Division of E. P. Dutton
2 Park Avenue / New York, New York 10016

Published simultaneously in Canada by Fitzhenry & Whiteside Limited, Toronto

First Edition
COBE
10 9 8 7 6 5 4 3 2 1

Library of Congress Cataloging in Publication Data

Aardema, Verna / Bimwili and the Zimwi

Summary / A Swahili girl is abducted by a Zimwi and told to be the voice inside his singing drum.
[1. Folklore — Tanzania — Zanzibar.]
I. Meddaugh, Susan, ill. II. Title.
PZ8.1.A213Bi 1985 398.2'1'096781 [E] 85-4449
ISBN 0-8037-0212-4 / ISBN 0-8037-0213-2 (lib. bdg.)

Bimwili and the Zimwi, A Tale from Zanzibar is retold from "Little Sister and the Zimwi" in *Tales for the Third Ear* (published by E. P. Dutton, Inc., 1969). The previous source is the story "The Children and the Zimwi" in *Swahili Stories,* by Kibaraka, Universities Mission Press, Zanzibar, 1896.

The full-color artwork was prepared using watercolor and colored pencils. It was then camera-separated and reproduced as red, blue, yellow, and black halftones.

One morning, when the mist was still pink from the sunrise, three sisters set out from a Swahili village to go to play by the sea. The path to the sea was long. And though the two older girls had walked it often, this was the first time for their little sister, Bimwili.

The big girls had not wanted to take her. Tete said, "Mama, Bimwili is too little to go so far!" And Tasha added, "Something is sure to happen to her!"

But Mama Hawa said, "If you don't take Bimwili, you may not go either."

So Bimwili got to tag along behind her big sisters. The path led them through jungles vibrant with the morning songs of birds and swamps noisy with the *wurrr, wurrr, wurrr* of frogs.

Finally they reached the sea. Huge breakers were rolling in, *she-OSH—she-OSH!* The two older girls waded in and began diving through the waves, while Bimwili played at the water's edge. She would follow the backwash, then run back with the next wave *t-lopping* at her heels.

Suddenly something that looked like a daytime moon came rolling in with a wave, and it tumbled at Bimwili's feet. "Ai!" she cried. "A shell! It's mine!"

Bimwili sat on a nearby rock to examine it. She ran her fingers around the bumpy ridge that spiraled to a peak. She held the smooth open side of it to her cheek. Then, to her surprise, she heard a soft SHHHHHH, like the sound of the sea, coming from inside it. She made up a song that she sang over and over:

I have a shell from out of the sea;
A shell the big wave gave to me.
It's pink inside like the sunset sky;
And in it you hear the ocean sigh.

After a while Bimwili put down the shell and went back to playing in the water.

When the sun was straight up in the sky, the girls set out for home. They had not gone far when Bimwili cried, "My shell! I forgot it! We must go back and get it!"

Tasha said, "Bimwili, I knew you would be a bother."

And Tete said, "Next time we come, we will find your shell again."

But Bimwili insisted on going back at once. And they let her go all by herself. Alone on the path, she was afraid. So she sang:

> I have a shell from out of the sea;
> A shell the big wave gave to me.
> It's pink inside like the sunset sky;
> And in it you hear the ocean sigh.

Bimwili was still singing when she reached the beach. And there, sitting on the rock where she had left her shell, was an ugly, old Zimwi! His face was creased like a shrunken gourd, and his long arms dangled down the sides of the rock. When he saw Bimwili, his wrinkles crinkled into a smile. He greeted her, "*Jambo,* Little Girl. How sweetly you sing!"

"*Jambo,*" said Bimwili hesitantly. "I want my shell that is there beside you."

"Sing for me first," said the Zimwi.

Bimwili began in a scared little voice: "I have a shell from out of the sea. . . ."

"No, no, no!" cried the Zimwi. "I can't hear you. Come closer and sing louder."

Bimwili obeyed. But the Zimwi said he still could not hear her. He made her sing over and over, each time coming closer.

At last she was so near, he flung out his long arms and caught her, GURUM! "Now I have you, my Little Singer!" he cried.

"Mama! Mama! Mama!" screamed Bimwili, as the Zimwi stuffed her into a big drum that he had beside him. Then he threw in the shell and fastened the drumhead in place.

Bimwili's crying gradually turned to sniffling, *hih, hih, hih.*

“Now,” said the Zimwi, “I have the only singing drum in the world. I shall be famous! And when I beat the drum, you, my Little Singer, will sing your song!” Then he picked up the drum and set out down a path.

Soon he came to a scatter of huts under some coconut trees. He went to the *baraza,* the meeting place. He said to the men there, “Gather the people together. I have a drum that can sing. Not *gum, gum, gum!* It sings a beautiful song. Cook me a meal, and I shall entertain you.”

While the food was being prepared, the Zimwi beat the drum. And a sad little voice inside it sang the song of the shell. The people were delighted. They let the Zimwi eat all he wanted. Then he took up the drum and set out for the next town.

Meanwhile the older girls arrived home.

"Where is Bimwili?" cried Mama Hawa.

They had to admit that they had let her return to the beach all by herself.

"Go back!" cried their mother. "How could you leave that little girl alone on the path!"

The girls hurried back down the path. They ran and walked, and walked and ran. At last they reached the sea. The tide was out! The beach was wide and bare! The only living things were the sand crabs skittering sideways, *guga, guga, guga.* The girls were terrified! Something bad had happened to Bimwili, and it was their fault.

When Tete and Tasha returned home without Bimwili, the whole village gathered under a mango tree. Their father, Hamasi, organized a search. It was evening, so the men set out with torches. They searched all night and for many days after that. At last they gave up.

During this time Bimwili was traveling with the Zimwi. It was uncomfortable living in the drum by day and sleeping on the scruffy mats of guest huts at night. She ate food from the jungle — bananas, coconut meat, and coconut milk. And each night her going-to-sleep song was the SHHHHHH of the sea in her shell.

Bimwili's only duty was to sing. She became bored with singing the same thing over and over, so sometimes she changed the words. And the Zimwi did not seem to notice.

After many days it happened that the Zimwi carried the drum into a village that encircled a mango tree. He went to the *baraza* and said to the men, "Gather the people together. I have a drum that can sing. Not *gum, gum, gum!* It sings a beautiful song. Cook me a meal, and I shall entertain you."

As the food was being prepared, one of the women asked, "Bwana Zimwi, do you want fish or fowl with your rice?"

Inside the drum Bimwili caught her breath. That was her mother's voice! This was her *own* village!

When the Zimwi beat the drum, she sang:

I have a shell from out of the sea;
A shell the Zimwi stole from me.
It's dark in here like the midnight sky;
If you listen you'll hear Bimwili sigh!

Now Mama Hawa was stirring the kettle. She did not hear the song. But Tete and Tasha heard! They gasped with delight. They hurried to their mother and whispered, "It's Bimwili! It's Bimwili singing in the drum!"

So when the Zimwi was about to eat, Mama Hawa gave him a water pot and said, "Here, go to the river yonder and fetch us some water."

And while the Zimwi was gone, Bimwili's father, Hamasi, opened the drum. There was his little girl, all curled up inside it, holding her shell. He lifted her out and put her into the arms of her mother. With tears of joy Mama Hawa carried her to their own hut.

There Tete and Tasha hugged Bimwili. And together the three sisters giggled over the happy ending to their strange adventure.

Meanwhile Hamasi scooped sand into the drum and put the top back on.

Now, after the Zimwi had eaten, Hamasi said, "Play for us once more before you go."

The Zimwi began to beat the drum. No song came from it. "Sing, drum, sing!" he scolded. But the drum would not sing.

The people laughed, *che, che, che!* They laughed so hard, they doubled over and slapped their thighs.

And the Zimwi took his drum and hastily left. When he had gone a little way, he said, "Little Girl, why didn't you sing for me?"

No one answered from inside the drum.

Angrily the Zimwi tore off the drumhead. "Ala!" he bellowed, as he saw how he had been tricked. Then, PAPO HAPO! He turned the drum into a pumpkin vine and himself into a huge All-Devouring Pumpkin.

The next day the three sisters set out down that path to look for food. When they saw the Pumpkin, Bimwili cried, "Oooo! Let's pluck it for our mother!"

The Pumpkin said, "There you are, my Little Singer! I'll pluck you!" And he came rolling after Bimwili, *b-long, b-long, b-long.*

Tete and Tasha each grabbed one of Bimwili's hands. They ran headlong with her back to the village—to the *baraza* where Hamasi and some other men were sitting.

"Hide us!" they cried. "The Zimwi has turned into a Pumpkin, and he is chasing us!"

The men hurried the girls into the council hut.

Soon the big Pumpkin came rolling in. "Have you seen my people?" he asked.

Hamasi said, "Are your people pumpkins?"

The Pumpkin growled, "They're in that hut. I see their tracks." And he scrambled toward the doorway.

"Aa-ii!" cried Hamasi, as he leaped between.

Then, KWAK! The Zimwi turned from a pumpkin into a sea gull! And he flew away. Over the jungles, over the swamps, back to the beach, he flew.

He alighted on the rock where he had caught Bimwili. And there the Zimwi changed back to his usual self. His long arms dangled down the sides of the rock. And his wrinkled face crinkled into a smile as he said in farewell, "*Kwaheri,* my Little Singer."

That evening, at moonrise, the people of the village gathered inside a circle of fires and told tales. And little Bimwili had a story to tell and a shell to show.

To the people the shell was amazing. They passed it from one to another, holding it to their ears. And one by one, they listened to the mysterious whisper of the sea—SHHHHHH!